Bigboots
the Spider

ANGELA McALLISTER

Illustrated by Jess Mikhail

OXFORD
UNIVERSITY PRESS

OXFORD
UNIVERSITY PRESS

Great Clarendon Street, Oxford OX2 6DP

Oxford University Press is a department of the University of Oxford.
It furthers the University's objective of excellence in research, scholarship,
and education by publishing worldwide in

Oxford   New York

Auckland   Cape Town   Dar es Salaam   Hong Kong   Karachi
Kuala Lumpur   Madrid   Melbourne   Mexico City   Nairobi
New Delhi   Shanghai   Taipei   Toronto

With offices in

Argentina   Austria   Brazil   Chile   Czech Republic   France   Greece
Guatemala   Hungary   Italy   Japan   Poland   Portugal   Singapore
South Korea   Switzerland   Thailand   Turkey   Ukraine   Vietnam

Oxford is a registered trade mark of Oxford University Press
in the UK and in certain other countries

Text © Angela McAllister 2007
Illustrations © Oxford University Press 2007

British Library Cataloguing in Publication Data
Data available

ISBN: 978-0-19-846094-7

3 5 7 9 10 8 6 4

Available in packs

Stage 9 More A Pack of 6: ISBN 978-0-19-846092-3
Stage 9 Class Pack: ISBN 978-0-19-846099-2
Guided Reading Cards also available:
ISBN: 978-0-19-915230-8

Cover artwork by Jess Mikhail

Printed in China by Imago

Paper used in the production of this book is a natural,
recyclable product made from wood grown in sustainable forests.
The manufacturing process conforms to the environmental
regulations of the country of origin.

1

Nothing scares me!

Spider played all day in the thorn
bush. He loved to swing on his
super-elastic thread.

'Look at me! I'm flying!'

All the bugs and beetles thought he
was a hero.

At home, Spider did kicks and spins.
'Watch this!' he cried.

'Very clever,' said Mum as she
untangled his legs. 'I wish you were
clever enough to find matching socks!'

'Who cares about socks,' scoffed
Spider. 'I can jump from the treetops!'

'I want to jump from the treetops, too!' said his little sister.

Spider laughed. 'Wait until you are big and brave like me.'

'Show off,' said his sister. She didn't like Spider's boasting, and she didn't believe his stories.

One day, Spider noticed a house on the other side of the thorn bush.

'Stay away from there,' warned Dad. 'That's where the monsters live.'

'What sort of monsters?' asked Spider.

'Gigantic ones,' said Dad, 'with hundreds of fangs!'

Spider wanted to take another look. 'Don't go!' cried the bugs and beetles. 'The monsters will grab you! They'll stamp on you with their gigantic feet!'

'I'm not afraid,' said Spider. 'Nothing scares me.'

'Don't go!'

2

The monsters' house

Spider was excited. He wanted to explore the monsters' house and have a real adventure.

So he crept through the thorn bush and tiptoed across the grass.

Suddenly a shadow fell over
Spider and he hid behind a leaf.

But it was only a sparrow.
Spider went on.
The monsters' house was very
quiet. Bravely, he stepped
inside...

The house was silent and still and
Spider went exploring.

He peeped in every room, but he
didn't see any monsters with fangs.
'Pah!' he said. 'This is boring.'
Spider sat down and scratched
his leg.

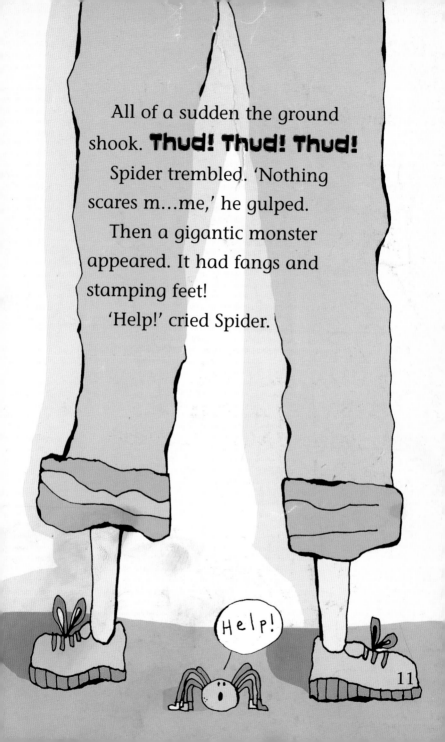

All of a sudden the ground shook. **Thud! Thud! Thud!**

Spider trembled. 'Nothing scares m…me,' he gulped.

Then a gigantic monster appeared. It had fangs and stamping feet!

'Help!' cried Spider.

Help!

The monster lifted its foot and Spider shut his eyes.

'HELP!' screamed the monster.
'A SPIDER!' It shook with fear and its fangs rattled. Then it turned white and ran away.

Spider was amazed.

When Spider got home, he told his family about the monster.

'*I* scared it off!' he boasted. 'It looked at me and ran away.'

'I want to see the monster, too,' said his sister.

'No,' said Spider. 'You'd be too scared. You're even afraid of teeny-weeny bugs!'

3

Bigboots

Spider's story spread all over the thorn bush. Little bugs and beetles loved the tale of Spider and the monster. By morning, he was famous.

Now Spider wanted more
adventures. He went back to the
monsters' house and he hid in the
plughole of the bath.

When another monster arrived,
Spider jumped out.

This monster was all pink, but it
screeched and ran away just like the
first one.

Spider had fantastic fun. Scaring
monsters was easy.

He climbed onto their pillows
and tickled their ears.

He jumped into their breakfast.

He swung under their noses.

He popped out of their shoes.

Spider had a great time.

Spider's mum and dad were
not happy.

'You are always late for tea,'
grumbled Mum.

'You're getting too big for your
boots,' warned Dad.

'**Bigboots!**' cried Spider's sister. 'I don't believe you've ever seen a monster. You're just making it all up!'

Spider grinned. 'You just wish you were brave like me,' he said.

4
Look out!

One morning, Spider marched
into the monsters' house but no one
was there.

He sat in the bath. He had a doze in
a shoe. Then he hung in the doorway,
but there was nobody to scare.

Suddenly, Spider saw his sister creeping across the doorstep! She had followed him to the monsters' house. She *was* brave like him, after all.

Spider was just going to call out and tell her to be careful. Then he froze.

Out of the shadows crept a
teeny-weeny bug. Spider was
TERRIFIED of teeny-weeny bugs!
He shook like a jelly.

'Look out!' he said in a tiny voice,
but his sister didn't hear.

The teeny-weeny bug
crept up behind Spider's sister.
   She took a step.
   So did the teeny-weeny bug.
   She took another step.
   So did the teeny-weeny bug.
   She turned around...

'Help!' screamed Spider's sister.

Suddenly, they heard,

'Thud! Thud! Thud!'

'The monsters are coming home,' cried Spider. 'Run!'

But his sister was so scared she couldn't move.

'I've got to save her,' thought Spider.

Then Spider remembered what his mother always said. 'Don't be afraid of teeny-weeny bugs. They are much smaller than you.'

Spider took a deep breath. He whizzed up to the top of the door.

'Watch out below!' he cried and he **swooped** down and grabbed hold of his sister.

Spider grabbed hold of his sister, swung her out of the door and onto the grass.

'Thanks,' she said. 'I didn't believe you were brave, but you *really* are!'

'Well, *you* were brave to follow me,' said Spider, proudly.

5

Nothing scares us!

Spider and his sister went home. She told everyone how he had saved her.

'You're not even afraid of teeny-weeny bugs,' she said. 'Are you?'

'They're so *small*,' said Spider with a wink. 'I don't bother being scared of them!'

'Spider is a hero!' cried all the bugs and beetles.

'My sister's brave too,' said Spider. 'She went into the monsters' house alone.'

'Yes, nothing scares *us*!' said Spider's sister. She smiled at him happily.

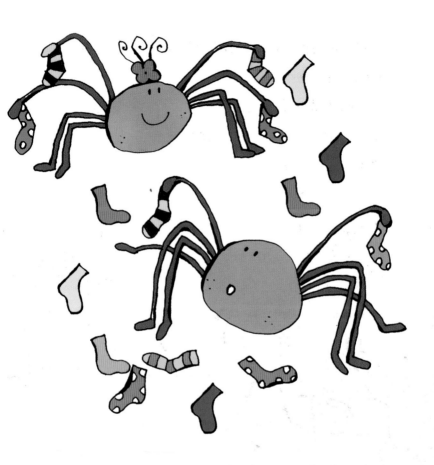

Next morning, Spider's sister helped
him find matching socks. Then he took
her to the thorn bush to play.

'Take care,' said Mum. 'Don't swing
too high.'

But they did! They swung
high, side by side. They were
brave and fearless together and
it was great!

When the teeny-weeny bug got
home, he told his family about
the spiders.

'I scared them off!' he boasted.
'Two of them!'

'I don't believe you,' said his sister.
'Next time, I'm coming with you!'

About the author

Lots of spiders live in my old
house. I like them but my
children are afraid, even
though spiders are so small.
I hope this story will help
them to be braver. After
all, it is the spiders'
house too!